A Splendid Chance

Flairs and Glairs
Publication House

"A Splendid Chance"

ISBN No: " 9789391302733"
1st Edition
Language – English and Hindi

Flairs and Glairs
Publication House
Regd. Under MSME Act.

Disclaimer

This is a work of fiction and solely represent the thoughts of the corresponding authors of the articles. Our editors have tried their best to edit the content of all the authors and check the plagiarism.

All the write-ups in this book are unique and are only published in this book.

In case any plagiarism or error is found, only the author is responsible alone, and not the publisher or the Compilers.

Cover Designing and Book Formatting
Shubham Shah and Ishani Agarwal

Acknowledgement

Dear Almighty, thank you for blessing me with the power and zeal to be able to complete this Anthology.

Also, Thank You dear parents, for trusting in me, and letting me work whenever I wanted. My family is the one who supported me for what I am today.

When it comes to th is, Anthology, I would like to start with Thanking the Co -Authors, without your help and support, I would have never been able to complete it.

Thank you all of you, for being there. Much Love to all of you. I am glad to see you all standing by me.

Co Author

Shubham Shah (Founder Flairs and Glairs)
Ishani Agarwal (Co-Founder Flairs and Glairs)
Shivangi Jaiswal (Compiler)

1. Samata Dey Bose
2. Parijat Chakraborty
3. Priyanka Bhattacharjee
4. Gaurav Thakur
5. Rutba Qayoom
6. Pavleen Bhatia
7. Sravani
8. Meenambiga Selvakumar
9. S.Sukruthi Meghamala
10. Akanksha Sinha
11. Afsar Shaikh

Shubham Shah

(Founder - Flairs and Glairs)

Shubham Shah, an entrepreneur at "Flairs & Glairs" a brand with dynamics in events organizing and cultural   educational pan INDIA, is a 26yrs old guy who recently has entered the digital platform of imprinting emotions. He has initiated with his own open mic platform to help budding poets and aspiring writers under his brand named as "Teekhe Zasbaaat"

He is a commerce graduate from the Bhagalpur City of Bihar. He states Writing has impersonated him since childhood and he has now been writing for over a decade!

Cooking, on the other hand, is his passion! He also mentions, trying out new things just tickles him!

When asked sir, Why SPICY EMOTIONS?

He smiled and added, "agar jasbaat teekhe na ho toh wo jasbaat kahan" Spices are all that blends! So do his words!

As a chef, he presents to you his dish! Hot and freshly served! Taste it! Feel it! Enjoy it! You can also find his writing in the Book "Teekhe Zasbaaat" and 50+ Co -authored anthologies.

With his passion to explore opportunities across Platforms, he is working with keen devotion and We wish him all the very best for his future ventures.

He is Featured in the International Magazine DeMode for his upcoming solo novel.

He is Approved by Ne8x for its Lit Fest, and is a Golden Star Awards 2020 Winner.

He is a India Book of Records Holder for his Anthology Satrang, and has the Grandmaster title by Asia Book of Records, for the same.

He has also been featured in Prabhat Khabar, Dainik Jagran, and a lot of other Newspapers in Bihar for his achievements.

He has been a proud co-author to

India Book Of Records (Title- Black)

World Book Of Records (Title -15 Wonders of Poetries)

India Book Of Records (Title - Aaina)

Vajra World Records Holder (Title - Gustakhi Maaf Hai)

High Range of Records Holder (Title - Gustakhi Maaf Hai)

Indian Book of Records

(Title - Road from Worst to Best)

Share your reviews on his

INSTAGRAM

@spicy_emotions
@shubham4shah
Or via email on

shubham2shah@gmail.com

To stay tuned to his work and opportunities follow his business Handles

INSTAGRAM   FACEBOOK   YOUTUBE

@flairsandglairs
@teekhezasbaaat

WEBSITE:

https://flairsandglairs.in/
https://flairsandglairs.com/

Ishani Agarwal

(Co-Founder - Flairs and Glairs)

Ishani Agarwal hails from the City of Joy, Kolkata.

She is the co -founder of her Community "Teekhe Zasbaaat" and Flairs and Glairs Publication.

Been a Compiler for 45+ Anthologies, she is in the process for more. Co-authored in 150+ Anthologies. She is a India Book of Records Holder, a Vajra W orld Records Holder, a High Range of Records Holder, an OMG Book of Records Holder, a Bravo Record holder, a Forever Star Book of World Records and an Indian Book of Records Holder.

Approved by Ne8x for its Lit Fest 2020, and Literary Icon 2020. Also a Golden Star Awards Winner 2020.

She has also been awarded with India Star Republic Award 2021, a part of She Awards by Awards Arc and Winner of Nari Samman 2021 by Literoma.

She is also selected as Best Achiever of the Year by AwardsArc and Most Challenging Compiler Award by Spectrum Awards.
She got her first solo Published,a solo Compilation consisting of first 750 contents of hers, titled "Hand That Burnt While Healing".

She has been featured by the National Magazine "Taree Zameen Par" with the title 'unstoppable'.
Also featured in the International Magazine DeMode for her upcoming solo novel, she is proud to write on social issues, and is happy with the love she is receiving.
Connect with her on Instagram: @Ishani_agarwal_quotes / @compilations_so_far

Shivangi Jaiswal
(Compiler)

Shivangi Jaiswal is a Content Writer from Kolkata. Executive Head at "Flairs & Glairs" brand with dynamics in events organizing and cultural educational pan INDIA. Organizer at "The Glittering Fables" Writing Community. She is a B. Com Honors graduate. Certified in Stocks & Short Selling as well as Certified in Digital Marketing student.
She is an Indian Book of Record Holder.

Approved by Ne8x for its Lit Fest 2020 for the Author of the Year 2020 and the Real Hero's Title 2020. Also, a Warrior of Change Awardee 2021.

Recently been awarded Writer of the year Award 2021 by Forever Star World book of Records.

She loves to bring smiles and happiness to many faces, so she is into social service.

Traveler, Teacher, Meditator, Dancer, Singer, Instrument Player. She loves to play guitar and harmonium. Also been awarded in many events for winning many categories Been a Public Speaker she has taken part in many events and nailed it. Been a great Advisor to many. She has also been crowned for winning Miss Great Podium 2020 Title in the category Modelling recently. Sports freak of Swimming and Badminton with a passion so strong. Since, past one year she has started her writing journey.

She writes so that many people can connect with their stories and get positive hopes. She thinks " Every story is unique so embrace yourself to the best". She is a writer by day and a reader by night. Been a Complier of 40+ Anthologies, and in process for more, also Co - authored 1 50+ anthologies. Shivangi is an old soul with young eyes, a vintage heart, and a beautiful mind."

You can follow her work:
Instagram
@the_knockingvibe
@house_of_compilations

If I Had Another Chance.

One chance that is all you get.
Don't lose it when it comes your way,
Make a good effort.

Sometimes life may be hard or sometimes it may be cruel.
Be aware!
Thorns will come by your way but don't fall.
Hold on! Decisions would be hard.
It might take a wrong way.

But when its wrong there are rights also.
You may lack in your faith, hold fear in your heart.
Don't worry your all problems will end.
A new path will come your way and it will be your own.

You have been given a second chance, smile and let
happiness enter.
Because everything happens for the best.
And remember you are worthwhile.

A Place Next to You.

A place of joy.
A place away from all sorrow and loneliness.

A place where two hearts beat as one
A place where two souls are together,
mending the broken hearts of one another.

A place in your arms.
A place of sweet abandon.

A place next to you giving light to the soul.
A place of moments of glad grace.

A place of glowing bars.
A place I want to spend my whole life.
A place so deep in dusk and dawn.

A Stranger I Wished To Know.

There is a shady shadow
that walks in the darkness makes
his way to live a broken life.
Mends his way to the needy
offers a shoulder to cry.
And wraps away everyone's
sorrows and sheds happiness
all over.
A stranger so pure, that walked
in the darkness to enlighten happiness.
Held, the hand of the weaken and
carefully saved them.
In the world of landscape
it brought regions of kindness.

Change What Is to Come

"NO" Still means "NO"
Some like it, some don't.
Why should I be scared of wearing short skirts?
Why should I be worried if I walk down alone?
Why can't I do things according to myself?
Why I need to change what I wear?
Instead of people changing their view.
Why should I have to be afraid every time?
Why should I look behind my back?
It's not my fault!
Men should learn not to attack.
Because "NO" means "NO"
Tell rapists "NOT TO RAPE".

Suffering

Suffering is a new era.
It is never enough,
nor it has any end.
It will harm you.
It does not care.
It lingers all around your body.
It will break you into pieces.
It finds a way in your life.
It weakens you slowly and led you to death.
It is a slow poison towards the end.
In the era of noise, someone was suffering in silence.

Samata Dey Bose

Samata Dey Bose is the founder of the entertainment E-portal Indiacafe24.com. She is an ex -banker and now a freelance content developer, book reviewer, author, poet, blogger, online interviewer, vedic astrologer, and also a passionate photographer. She compiled books under her banner Indiacafe24 and remained part of different anthologies. She won several awards for literary achievements. She has a keen interest in art and craft and loves traveling besides having other social involvements. In short, she is a lady with colorful dreams and sure to achieve each one of them one day.

Kahani Rajmata Ki Aka Warrior Queen of Malwa Ahilyabai Holkar

Chondi is a small village of Jamkhed, Ahmednagar of Maharashtra. In the year 1725 on 31st May, a girl was born to Mankoji Rao Shinde and his wife. He named her dotting daughter Ahilya. Mankoji Shinde was serving as the Patil or chief of Chondi village, at the time of her daughter's birth. During that time education for women and the girl -child was something very weird even to discuss. But Mankoji Rao Shinde was known for his great vision and made every arrangement at his home in the village for educating his daughter and encouraged her to read and write.

That was just the beginning of a story, and that later turned into a glorified historic episode to encourage many women to think beyond the established norms of society. Mankoji's daughter, Ahilya, was born with no royal background, and so when she made an entry in the pages of Indian History, many thought it was just by a twist of luck. She grew up with a different set of ideologies, which were difficult to witness among the women of that period. How Ahilya managed to engrave her name in golden letters in Indian historic chapters is something very important for me to narrate. Two important men in her life believed and witnessed the spark in the little girl. First was her father while the other was the then ruler of the Malwa territory, Shri Malhar Rao Holk ar. Malhar Rao Holkar's first meeting with Ahilya took place when she was busy serving the poor in the temple premises of her village. He found the girl to be different from others. He was on his way to Pune and had a small halt at Chondi when he came acro ss this girl of only 8 years.

He found that the girl all the qualities desired in a future queen. For Malhar Rao, Ahilya appeared to be a bold woman, who could also be a caring queen for the Praja (people of the ruling territory). So without wasting any time, he asked for the girl's hand from Mankoji for his son Khanderao Holkar. The proposal was quite shocking for the girl's family but getting such a royal proposal was something that he could not deny. Finally, Mankoji Rao agreed and Ahilya got married to   the prince of Malwa territory Khanderao Holkar in the year 1733 at the age of 8.

For the current queen and wife of Malhar Rao Holkar, it was initially very difficult to accept a village girl with no royal background to be her daughter-in-law. But the little girl's strong persona, devotion, caring, and sober nature made even the queen to fall in love with her bahu rani (daughter -in-law) within a very short time. Ahilya's relation with her young husband was more like that between two naughty friends than that between a husband and wife. The queen used to remain worried about the future of the couple and made continuous efforts to mingle Ahilya in the royal eco -system. But Ahilya was Ahilya and she was in no way ready to be a common girl instead of being a wo man of substance. Slowly and steadily, like her visionary father-in-law, the other members of the king's palace experienced the unique and endearing qualities in the girl. With time the relationship of Ahilya and Khanderao became stronger and the couple was blessed with two kids.

She remained outspoken if she found anything unethical or wrong in the court of justice which was presided over by her father-in-law. Many including the queen were not happy with this behavior of Ahalya, but Malhar Rao usually gav   e importance to her views and this impacted his judgment in the court many times. All these were signs of a visionary queen of the future, which in the later part proved to be true.

But her married life was not a blissful one and she lost her husband at the young age of 29 years only. Khanderao breathed his last when he was killed in the battle of Kumbher in 1754. As per the custom of that time, after her husband's death, the wife had to become sati and sacrifice her life. Ahilya was ready to accept this custom but king Malhar Rao Holkar decided to prevent his daughter-in-law from becoming sati and continued to support her as a father figure. However, destiny was not in favor and Ahalya visualized the falling of the kingdom after the death of Malhar Rao Ho lkar in the year 1766. As per the royal traditions, it was only the son or grandson of the king who could ascend to the throne. So it was Ahilya Bai's son, Male Rao, who took charge of the throne after his grandfather's death. The next blow of fate was unbearable for Ahilya Bai when within a few months of ascending to the throne, Male Rao died on the 5th of April in 1767. This created a complete vacuum throughout the kingdom as no male member was left to take control. For a common woman, life would have com e to a complete standstill after losing her husband, father-in-law, and only son, one after the other. But as already mentioned Ahilya Bai was a woman of substance and she took full control of her grief and didn't allow her sorrows to impact the administra tion of her kingdom. That was the beginning of the saga of the Warrior Queen of Malwa, Ahilyabai Holkar. She forwarded her petition to the Peshwa to take over the royal administration under her belt. It was in the year 1767 on the 11th of December that she adorned the throne of Malwa as its ruler. A certain segment of people within the kingdom was against the decision of her taking charge of the throne. During this time, it was the Holkars army that gave her complete support and stood by her side as a mark of approval of her leadership. Within a year of taking charge of the kingdom, history witnessed the power of a bold and brave warrior queen saving Malwa by defeating its enemies in the battle. Equipped with a sword in hand she proved to be an inspiring com   mander for her army leading it into one battle after another on the back of her favorite elephant.

Her advisor for military decisions was Subhedar Tukojirao Holkar. He was her father-in-law's adopted son and she found him to be the perfect person to take charge as the head of the army on the battlefield. She also created a 500 -woman army under her and they were trained using a European method by a French general named Dadurnec. This army had a big cannon known as 'Jwala'. In addition to being a brave   -heart queen, Ahilya Bai also came to be known as a brilliant visionary politician. Witnessing the fact that the Peshwa was facing difficulty in controlling the agenda of the British, she penned down a letter to him in 1772. In her letter, she mentioned that enemies like tigers can be killed when you have a strong eye and the intellect of a shikari. Things are different when your target is a bear and it will get killed only when it gets hit straight on the face. If one falls prey to the powerful hold of the bear, it will kill one just by tickling. The Britishers are like the bear and so it will be difficult to put them down.

Under her leadership, people witnessed the expansion of a small village to a glorious city known as Indore now. She ruled for 30 long years and devoted herself to constructing several roads and forts. She also contributed to hosting many festivals and made countless donations in different Hindu temples. What made this queen different from the other women of her era? It was her treatment of the rich and poor as equals. She ensured justice was not denied to anyone simply based on their economic status in society. Courts were set up at various places for delivering justice in a short time and at a low cost.

There is one story worth sharing about   her that delivers the lesson of maintaining equality in judgment for all. Once

Malojirao, son of Ahilyabai was driving his chariot in Malwa and a young, almost newborn calf came in his way. The mother cow was at a small distance from the calf and standing on the roadside. The chariot hit the calf, which got injured brutally and lost its life right there. Without waiting to see what happened to the calf, Malojirao went on in his chariot and this was witnessed by the common men around. The cow's eyes were filled with tears on witnessing the death of her child in front of its eyes and it sat close to the calf on road.

After some time, Rani Ahilyabai also passed by the same route and witnessed the dead calf and its mother. It took a few seconds for her to under stand what exactly might have happened to the calf. Taking note of the case details her heart broke down realizing the pain of the mother cow. She ordered to tie hands of Malojirao and ordered his death penalty by hitting him with the chariot. All arrangements were done unwillingly by her people but the Baghiwan(chariot driver) declined the order of the queen stating he couldn't do it. When no one was ready to carry out her orders, the queen herself drove the chariot and started approaching the spot where Malojirao was tied in the middle of the road.

Complete silence spread over the crowd observing the scene and when she was just about to hit her son, that mother cow came in front of the chariot. Despite removing her several times, the cow came in front of the chariot again and again. It intended to protect the prince. People started saying that God was taking a critical test of the queen's judgemental power and sent the cow for the same. One of the ministers then requested the queen to stop and said that even the cow doesn't want this to happen to the child of another mother like her. The act of the cow indicated that she is requesting the queen for mercy for the prince. Ahilyabai is still well known for this strict

judgment and the spot is popular even toda y in the name of Aada Bazaar.

The Holkar Rani also earned a name for her contribution towards decorating and modifying various religious sites like Kashi, Somnath, Gaya, Ayodhya, Hardwar, Kanchi, Mathura, Avanti, Dwarka, and Jaganathpuri. These are only some of the names based on the records of Bharatiya Sanskritikosh. She remained a religiously tolerant queen. Despite being a Hindu by religion, she openly accepted and welcomed the followers of the Muslim religion. She allotted space in her kingdom for the Muslims and that too in Maheshwar and monetarily supported the construction of mosques. Maheshwar was her capital and was known as a cultural hub for literature, music, art, and industrial achievements. She welcomed gems like Moropant a Marathi poet, Shah ir Anantaphandi as well as Khushali Ram a Sanskrit scholar. Her visionary power in terms of business and creativity remained supreme. During her reign craftsmen, sculptors, as well as artists, got due recognition for their work and with handsome pay. She w as the pioneer in opening the textile industry in her capital city. In her time the cloth merchants created their best pieces of clothes and expanded their trade beyond the boundaries. During her rule, the farmers remained happy and self - sufficient in life. Her public presence was a daily affair where she used to hear the grievances of her people and try to resolve them in the best possible way. She was a queen who remained ready to serve her people whenever required by them.

Once Annie Besant penned down about Ahilyabai Holkar and mentioned that during her reign the roads were filled with shady trees. In addition, she contributed openly to support the poor, homeless, and orphans.

The biggest blow in her life came when her only daughter decided to accept the curse of sati pratha by sacrificing her life in the funeral pyre after the demise of her husband Yashwantrao Phanse. Ahilya Bai breathed her last at the age of 70 and her throne was taken over by Tukoji Rao Holkar I the commander in chief of her ministry.

These days we talk about women empowerment but what exactly it stands for was taught by this great queen of Malwa several decades back. She is undoubtedly an inspiration for the woman of the 21st century and there is a lot more to learn from her life story. She is a true example of a modern woman who knows when to be bold and strict, when to be fierce and when to shower the fragrance of love and care on her people. Despite so many difficulties in her life, she remained adamant and strong as she knew the responsibility of her people was on her shoulders.
Indian history is proud to have such an inspirational queen whose life is like a golden lesson not just for women but for men too.

Parijat Chakraborty

Parijat Chakraborty - born and brought up in the land of Assam is a passed-out student from Department of English who has an extensive love for poetry. She started writing at the age of 16 and very soon she became a part of Flairs and Glairs as a co-author. She's an animal activist by nature and is also associated with an NGO and believes in helping the needy and the underprivileged. Also has a strong urge to help the needy in the future with some portion of her income.

Together Forever

Alluring face with a lively smile
Worth seeing from a mile
Strides to the path of joy
Provokes one and all to enjoy

Every little thing of you matters
Feels so immense to let me utter
The delighted endless talks
 The pleasing united walks

You make me feel special
Mounting up in being a rebel
We love we laugh we fight
Still and all you hold me tight

With intent to make every moment count
Will let entire phase to flaunt
A vow to remain constant
Gathering every exceptional moment.

Agony Of Love

All I wished to get back the old you
Instead, you chose to be the same you
Still been longing for the lost love
The one you offered from all above

Craving for you to change
Seeming as everything derange
I loved you dearly, I love you still
In my heart you hold a place that no one can ever fill

Though will not be able to narrate
Now all I can do is just wait.

A Beauty to Adore

Beauty is her angry red cheeks
Beauty is her silent taunt tricks
The way she screams
The way she beams

How to define
Her essence with shine
Making every moment special
Caring every belonging essential

Pretty lady full of wisdom
Oh, Mom you are awesome.

The Changing Bond

From strangers to friends, friends to confidante
How can it so easily end
Where's the fun, where's the joy
Don't let it crash like a toy

That crazy late night talks
That sassy long walks
Distance kept us apart
Still you grasp a place in my heart

Somewhere and somehow the bond changed
The changed things need to be arranged.

Her Never Ending Love for me

From her womb to her lap
Stillness with a peaceful nap
Loaded heart by offering pamper
Holding on all my temper

Thrived with committing mistakes
Still was excused for my sake
In a move to make her proud
Letting her to cheer up loud

Will wind with full effort
Knowing I have that support.

Priyanka Bhattacharjee

Priyanka Bhattacharjee - born and brought up in the land of hills, valley and tea gardens Assam; is an English teacher by profession. It's her immense love for language and literature that makes her live a passionate life. With a positive outlook towards life, she is inclined to reading, cooking and writing. She is interested in music and learning new things. With an intention to motivate her students, she took to writing inspirational quotes and poems. She has already been a co - author of a couple of beautiful anthologies like 'Life-An ineffable journey', 'January Proposals', 'Hidden Wish Project' and is now working on a few more projects. Writing provides food to her soul. She now dreams to publish a book as a sole author.

What is Love?

A sweet emotion that makes you realize your worth.
Love is an ocean where you need to dive in,
Love is an emotion which we need to engross in.
Love is what gives us our identity.
Love brings out the best in us eradicating every negativity.
Love never lets you give up,
Even when life seems to be tough.
Love is eternal, love is a bliss.
Love is a blessing, a messenger of peace.
Love gives you the hope for a new beginning,
Love makes you understand the miracle of living.

The Precious Bonds

What a wonderful term it is-
Which we call 'Relationship'.
Born even before our birth,
Relations are what that make our life worth.
Right in her womb,
We build a strong bond with our mom.
Gradually in nine months
Making our bond firmer,
We are born to come across many new relations
Which with due time gets familiar.
Every relation has its own significance,
Be it our parents or spouse,
Offspring or some special acquaintance.
Emotions would have breathed their last,
Had relations been left outcast.
It's a relation which makes a house our home,
It's a relation which makes
our heart acknowledge every emotion.

A Promise till Forever

Promises are easy to be made.
An assurance is so easy to be given.
'I will be there for you'
It's so easy to be spoken.
But, can you make a promise
To never break your promise?
Can you give the assurance?
That you would be my constant
Whether it's my halcyon days
Or days when everything seems imperfect?
Promise me that you will be by my side,
Make me feel everything would be alright.
Let's promise together-
We will never judge each other.
No matter what's the cause.
Let's promise to keep every promise
Today and forever.

The Real Fighter

They call her strong physically,
Some say she is brave mentally,
She has the strength to bear every atrocity,
She can fight against any instability.

Yes, she is a real warrior,
Inspite of being scarred by your brutality,
She never let herself be shattered.
She stands up repeatedly like a true fighter.

She let her tears flow as abundantly as her laughter,
And that's what declares her a true fighter.

Can We Start Over Again?

Life was so irrelevant till I found you as my soulmate.
You are my sole need, we were meant to meet.
You are the brightest star of my night sky.
You are my wings which let me swore high.
My heart loses its beat everytime you are away.
You are that smile on my face which never let me cry.
It's years since we are together, but I want you forever.
Will you be my strength when I fall weak?
Will you let me be the voice who can read the language your
heart speaks?
Let's get old together-
Will you hold me strong if I stumble ever?

Gaurav Thakur

His Name is Gaurav Thakur; He is from Araria district, Bihar; He is a mechanical engineer by profession. He likes to write Emotions, Feelings and State of mind through Poetry, Shayri, Gazal and quotes. He started writing in 2019 and till now he had written almost 850 quotes.

1) साथ दिल का !

वो दिल हीं क्या !? जो कभी टूटा ना हो !
वो वादा हीं क्या जो झूठा ना हो !
वो किश्मत हीं क्या जो फूटा ना हो !
और वो साथ हीं क्या !? जो कभी छूटा ना हो !

2) :- बेवफाई !

बेवफा कोई नहीं है साहब : सबके हैं यहाँ ; अपने-अपने सपनें !
समय वो दर्पण है , जिसने दिखा दिया है : कि कौन थे गैर ; और
कौन हैं वो ! जो कभी हो नहीं सकते मेरे अपने !

3) :- चांद को पैगाम !

चांद भी जानता है कि बस चार दिन की है : बची उसकी जवानी !
जी भर जाये , तब तक : करले पूरी वो भी ; अपनी मनमानी !
लगता है जैसे कि , जब खत्म होगी उसकी सारी नादानी !
तब कहीं जा शुरू हो सकेगी : हमारी कहानी !

4) :- मिलन की जतन !

मिलो तो इस तरह कि , हंसी में छिपा गम ढूंढ़ लो !
बात भले चाहे दिल की करो : पर यूँ हो सिरकत ; कि मन छू लो !

5) :- रात़ बिखरी दिऌ में   !

रात़ की राख़ बिखऱ गयी ; दिऌ में   !
आंखों की जमीं पानी : उतऱ गयी, उस़ सूखी अंधेरी झीऌ में   !
जो बरसती आंखों औऱ सूखे होटों से : हमनें लगाई गुहाऱ ; संभालने की   !
वक़्त़ ने कहा , बस़ तूम़ हीं नहीं साहब़ : मैं खुद़ भी हूँ ; बड़ी मुश्किऌ में   !

6) :- प्याऱ से मुलाकात़   !

अगऱ प्माऱ मुझे मिलने आता !
तो वो भी प्याऱ को भूऌ जाता , औऱ बेफिक्री के नशेमऩ में   !
बेपरवाह़ याऱ उसे मिऌ जाता   !

7) :- चूऱ हुआ़ गुरूऱ   !

चूऱ हो चलें हैं : अब़ तो ; उनके भी गुरूऱ   !
कुछ़ यूँ करिश्माई थी वो : इश्क़-ऐ-शुरूऱ   !
ना वो समझ़ सके , कि था निर्दोष़ कौऩ औऱ ना हीं हम़ समझ़ पाये : कि था आखिऱ वो किसका कुसूऱ   !
जो कभी हो दिलोंमऩ से ख्वाहिश़ : बात़ पूरी करने की ; तो कभी दूबारा मिलना जरूऱ   !

8) मरहम़ !

आओ़ मरहम़ बऩ जायें हम़ : एक़ दूसरे के घाव़ पऱ   !
मत़ रखना तूम़ , कोई भी बंदिशें ; अपने स्वभाव़ में   !
जब़ हालत़ एक़ सी हीं है : दिलों की ; दोनों के हीं   !
फिऱ क्या रखा है : पहले आप़ , पहले आप़ के भेदभाव़ में   !

9) :- जब़ वापस़ आओ़   !

जब़ वापस़ आओ़ , तो वहीं कहीं छोड़कऱ ; अपने सारे इलज़ाम़ आना
!
मनमर्जी में भी , इतनी नियत़ हो : कि फिऱ कभी ना रिश्ते पऱ अपनी
; विराम़ लगाना   !

10) :- जायका ईश्क़ का   !

यूँ ना रखो इरादे : कि एक़ झटके में चख़ लोगे तूम़ जायका ; मेरी
दिवानगी के मसालों का   !
दिखे होंगे कुछ़ रंग़ तूम्हें , मेरी आशिकी की औऱ देखना है बांकी ;
तूझे हऱ धंग़ दिलवालों के

11) :- मामला दिल्लगी का   !

तूम्हारे साथ़ सब़ सुलझायें : मामला दिल्लगी का ; पऱ सामने तो आओ॒ !
यो होकऱ ओझ़ल : बेवक्त़ हीं ; मेरे गले ना पड़ जाओ॒   !
आना हो तो : फायदे से नहीं ; कायदे से आओ॒   !
जो हो कभी महसूस़ : कि बेईमानी का सारा जिम्मा हमारा था ; तो जिस़ तरह़ हो मुमकिऩ , उस़ हिसाब़ से मामले को सुलझाओ॒   !

12) :- गजल़ 01 (लम्हों की पुकाऱ)!

हऱ लम्हां तुझको हीं पुकारूँ   ;
कहाँ रहता है अब़ , मतवाले को इतनी फूरसत़   !
होकऱ गुलाम़ आवारगी का :
सांप़ बऩ तुझसे लिपट़ जाऊँ , नहीं है बची ; अब़ ऐसी कोई हसरत़ !
जाने कितनी हीं हसीऩ रातों को :
बेरंग़ हीं गुजाऱ गये हम़ ; बदल़-बदल़ के करवट़   !
वो करिश्माई किरदाऱ आपके हीं थे :
जो कऱ चल़ है , पाने-खोने की मोह़ को हमसे ; अब़ रूकसत़   !

13) :- गज़ल 02 (इल्जाम़-ऐ-कत्लैआम़)!

जो हऱ बाऱ , बस़ तेरी हदों को ललकारे ;
उसे इम्तिहाऩ कहते हैं !
औऱ जो बेवजह़ हीं , तुझ से आकऱ चिपट़ जाये :
उसे इल्जाम़ कहते हैं !
भूल ना सका जिसे एक़ पल़ को ;
हऱ मतवाला आशिक़ , उसे इंतकाम़ कहते हैं   !
जाने कितनी हीं बाऱ , उडाये गये परखच्चे हमारे ;
पऱ जो कभी इऩ लबों से नहीं हुआ़ रूकसत़ , उसे मुस्काऩ कहते हैं
!
कभी पढ़ जो सको इऩ आंखों को तुम़ मेरी ; तो जो धरोहऱ हमनें
इसमें छिपाये रखा है , उसे तूफाऩ कहते हैं !
ऐतवाऱ तेरे हऱ फैसलों पऱ इतना है भोले : कि जो कैद़ है , मेरी
कलम़ के स्याही में ; उन्हें हम़ अपनी जाऩ कहते हैं !

Rutba Qayoom

Her name is Rutba Qayoom, resident of   Kashmir. Currently pursuing law degree from the University of   Kashmir. She is very passionate about writing and usually writes on social issues, motivation etc. She has already worked as a Coauthor in couple of anthologies, now she has joined hands with Flairs and Glairs publication as a Coauthor.

Forever Care

Each one is unique and needs affection
We all are humans with no scope of perfection.
Hatred, Jealousy, Selfishness are our attributes.
One should be pardoner and pay tributes.
Lover should be skilled in patience.
As beloved is nested in soul and needs attention.
One should be honest and fidel in relation.
Tale must be pellucid and masterpiece to creation.
Pledge should be for here and there.
Loving, Alluring and Forever Care.

The Eye- Opener

I freed you from every bondage of love.
I freed you from every expectation of love.
I freed you from every promise you made.
I freed you from everything whether it was contract or trade.
I answered every conspiracy with honesty and understanding.
I countered every difficulty with wisdom and patience.
I stood straight by holding my principles tightly.
I stood smiling by dropping my tears slightly.
Thanks for teaching me truths of life.
Honesty, Fidelity and Loyalty jewels of my existence.
Acquiring these principles turned my life meaningful.
I will always be your well-wisher and thankful.
Person with Golden Heart which I today possess.
Name which you used to call me Richie and Princess.

(3)

Advice to youth;

With age, time changed, we are now   civilized and honored beings of society, we enjoy luxurious lifestyle   but unfortunately, it's only superficial development. We actually are empty vessels. We lack peace, solace and   happiness. As we move forward, after fulfilling our aims and dreams, we as humans solely focus on how to get married and how to be happy in our future life. Here, be careful, choose wisely don't be haste as this one decision will determine the complexion of your life. My dear female friends, don't get attracted to luxurious lifestyle or handsome figure instead choose someone who actually wants to accept you whole heartedly, with whom you can share both bright and eclipsed part of your soul. Same is for male friends, don't choo se someone who is beautiful by looks give preference to beautiful and caring soul. Someone who knows how to make you happy in times of despair, who will support and encourage you to follow your passion.

 "Choose morals over models"

(4)

Scorching rays of Sun pains, us and Soothing scene of Sunset pleases us. Fortunately, both are the attributes of same. If divine source can't please us all the time how can a human full of faults. Loyalty should be enough to keep someone.

(5)

You can't win my soul with resplendent beauty and charming faces. These things not matter to me. Courageous soul, Detriment attitude, Impeccable manners will make you mine.

Pavleen Bhatia

pavleenbhatia/piquapoetry
"Words are magic in the hands of those who can wield them to fight their inner battles."
Writes poetry to bring out stifled feelings from the heart, and also to express extreme emotion.
A Doctor of English Literature in the making.

A Divine Embrace

Her day passed in tranquility
But, at night she felt emotionally wrecked
Because he had told a distant past tale
She listened closely as her mouth twitched with uneasiness
But a hawk's eye had he
Who identified the twitch in a moment?
He grew soft
His eyes brimming with love for her
He tried to console her with his words
Unaware that she was already consoled by the look in his
eyes
She still couldn't utter a word
Tears ebbed and flowed
He wiped away each tear thinking what wrong he'd have
done
But the thought that continuously played on repeat in her
head was
I know
I know
I can see it in your eyes
No words
No words
But the look in your eyes
Tells a thousand tales without you uttering a word
She cried happy tears
Because deep down in her heart she knew
She was his world

A Butterfly Dream

A beautiful butterfly with maple leaves all over it
Which dripped of syrup if it sat on you
Came flying one day and perched on my ring finger
It made my heart and soul drip in its syrup
A sweet syrup
Which I'd rather taste once in my lifetime before dying
And O a Blake
And O a Wordsworth
And O a Shelley
I'll sit beside a mountain, a lake, a forest, a beach
And, feel the joy and shed the pain through the wings of that
magical butterfly again.

My Beau

How can I say what I feel for you?
My heartbeat multiplies tenfold when I see you
Those almond shaped twinkling eyes hide behind a frame.
That dance with an angelic moonlight waltz.
Every time they're happy they dance like in a childlike never-
ending trance.
Your L shaped nose curves beauti   fully carefully crowning
your mole in regal aesthetic.
Your moustache upholds a divine name of a princely Sikh.
Flushing dimples hide behind its spiraling support.
Cheekbones white as snow, turn volcanic red when anger
flows.
A beard walking along the chiseled jawline.
He isn't just prodigious in appearance but is better than a
Machiavellian "Prince".
His heart beats for everyone but himself.
Careful critical consideration he offers all.
Opinions are as apt as the eyes of logic can see.
His heart is golden since within it resides purity, innocence
and naivete.
Matters of the heart are new to him.
But the way his heart beats he could drown oceans with his
sentiment.

Emotions V/S Diamonds.

Emotions are treasures bigger than jewels Bringing joy and tears at the same time How wonderful how breath taking they make us feel They differentiate us from a machine Emotions are treasures bigger than jewels They make ou r heart dance with nervousness in plight They make joy rekindle on a lonely night Some people they hold memories of whom we can't lay out of sight   Emotions are treasures bigger than jewels They can make a fragile woman of low birth and a stout woman of high birth's heart aflutter Without the thunder of divisions of social class Emotions are treasures bigger than jewels They place a heavy burden on the hearts of the ones Who see their children grow Who see their children go Out in the beautiful world Say, can a diamond stir these feelings Say, can a gold coin stir these meanings Within the depths of our soul?

The New Disease.

He says he's suffering/He says the disease is taking a toll on him/He says his family is unwell from this new disease/He says he has stress, anxiety and too much to think of/He says he needs a long holiday/ (New Para) It's been days since his family recovered/It's been days but they are surrounding themselves with the devil/ It's been days but with each passing day fear clasps him tighter and tighter in his fists/It's been days but his frame of mind is tangled up like the twisted knots on a shoe lace/(New para) I see each of my family members caged by the disease each day/I've seen them suffer but they've got hope and the spiri t of a true Sikh Warrior/I see the disease taking a toll on them but they know in their hearts they'll beat it/I see my family looking at a greener tomorrow, forgetting the suffering g of today/ I see them galloping like a horse through these days of chaos to reach a safe space/(new para) A simple safe space like the Philosopher's Stone/A simple safe space like the Kirpan of a Singh/A simple safe space where you can be if you only believe/A simple safe space known only to the heart and soul

Sravani

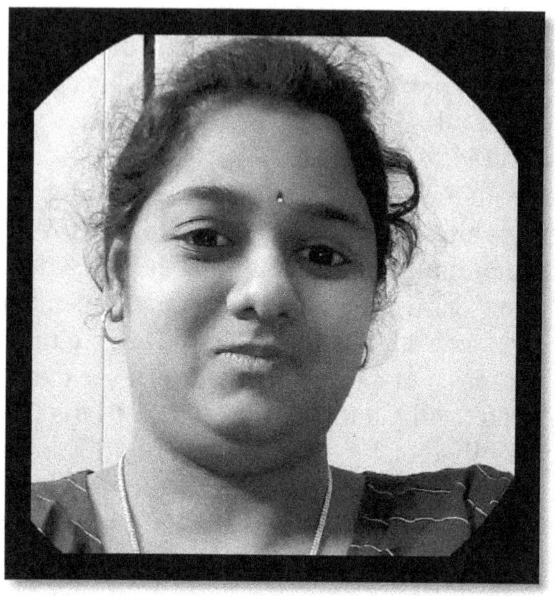

Sravani is a passionate writer, writing is her first and last love, because only for writing there is heart in her place. she loves to help budding writers, compiler of one anthology which was published recently and presently working on two anthologies one is aiming for the record.

She is also a community head of Jaziel -Inks which is like a second family to her.

Her besties are her inspiration for entering this writing world.

If My Phone Is a Human:

My phone's pov
If I am a human being like my owner,
I would definitely ask my owner to first remove my back
cover (laughing).
Jokes a part (serious expression)
If am a human being,
I will give one day class to my owner,
For using me from morning till night,
not at all giving me a little bit of rest.
My owner will be giving me rest when my stomach i.e., my
battery is low.
Until then I will be in her hands itself, poor me!
Punches me always as I am some boxing bag to her
Such a naughty girl she is!

Its Tears

It started to cry,
Because of having a low battery,
And because of the punches by me on her keyboard.
But why its hurting me seeing its tears,
May be Because it became a part of my life,
I consoled my heart,
And kept her in charge.

My Design (Phone's Pov)

I started to look at my back cover through a mirror, which was beautifully designed by the designers.

But then my back cover, my back design is wonderful and stunning and the color white which was used by the designers made me more beautiful.

Meenambiga Selvakumar

MeenambigaSelvakumar hails from Panruti. she is 21 years old girl. She pursuing her master degree in literature at Villupuram. she finished B. A in Theivanai Ammal college for women. She loves to write poems and quotes. she published paper on the topic Asian literature and she participated in seminars. she likes to do sudoku and she got first prize in that. she talented in puzzles. she likes her parent very much. She also has insta id meename19 and with__my__quotes.

Hello...Hello...I'm Your Mobile Speaking

I am proud to be a mobile of you
Sometimes your smooth fingers crossed me
It is like huge relaxation for me
I do not worry about my safety when in your hand

My dress is in favorite color pink
You used for long times
Please change new pink dress for me
I feel something happy when in your hand

Your contact list made me enthusiastic
Your friends list is more and more
WhatsApp stickers are very funny
WhatsApp status filled with your motivational quotes

I feel sad because you do not have any songs
I feel happy when I hear your sweet voice
I feel enthusiastic when I have a memory of you
I feel most beautiful with you.

S.Sukruthi Meghamala

Dad's Lil Princess and Mom's World
I am a song bird in the world of Telugu Vocals.
Now I'm working over writings..So that,people get knowing
me...It's not my Passion But,situations made me to write
poems..
Finally,
This is S.Sukruthi Meghamala Srivatsa,studying Degree final
year from Gattepalli village,Peddapalli district,
Telangana,India

Sky Is Your Limit

Not grace,
but only character
can make a person high;

But a mistake may lead
to one's down fall

As a high fort stands
boasting that
I'm Strong

But where that strength
came from??
The Secret behind is unity

No Pains, No Gains

A sprout pierced
through the earth
Do you know? asked the Sky,

The grain burries dead
Before, it can live again

Work hard.
to achieve your Goal
Then you fetch fruits of your labour.

Moon and me

I love you
really, I love you
from the bottom of my heart

Loving you is non sensical
As a part of your heart
How can I say that?
I love you

I am you,
You are me
There is no difference

We Are One

A Wonderful Dream

OH! I am swimming to pick
 a red lotus flowers
That blossomed in the middle
of a peaceful lake

There came some water birds
I wondered when a white swan
brought the lotus and presented me

My eyes twinkled
like Morning Stars

A New Life onto the Earth

After 9months of long waiting,
A cute baby born crying;

Father couldn't believe it...
Because,he was excited...
But,Mother felt extreme happiness...

When she opened her eyes,
After an excruciating pain,
She kissed baby's cheek...

Unknowningly,babe touched her mother's face,
with her smooth little hands...
Mother closed her eyes in ecstacy...

Akanksha Sinha

Akanksha Sinha is Banker by   profession, writer as passion. She is daughter of Mr. Mukesh Kumar and Mrs. Shikha Sinha. Lives in Patna,Bihar . She loves to portrait feelings by her poetry and quotes,she likes travelling and capturing moments. Heart healer by birth. She is coauthor of 25+ anthology. She loves to feel the nature. She is passionate &ambitious for her work.

वादा

जिन्होंने किया था कभी वादा हर पल में साथ निभाने का
आज उन्हे हमारा हाल भी पूछने का वक्त नही मिलता

तनहा जीने का भी अपना ही मजा है जनाब
वक्त पे भले कोई साथ ना हो
किसी के दिल तोड़कर जाने का डर नही होता

हँसते निगाहों में भी आंसुओं का शैलाब होता है
मुस्कुराते ओठों पर भी दर्द का पैगाम होता है
कोई इसे जरा समझ कर तो देखे
किसी को कुछ भी कह देना बहुत आसान होता है

मोमबत्ती की तरह पिघलती है जिन्दगी
गमों की आग में जलती है जिन्दगी
ठोकर लगे तो गम नहीं करना
क्यों कि ठोकर लग कर ही बदलती है जिन्दगी

जिन्दगी जब घाटे में चल रही हो
तो जरा सम्भल कर रहे जनाब
बहुत से लोग बैठे है इसका सौदा करने के लिए

कोई भी रास्ता आसान नही होता
मुश्किलों से डर कर जीवन का नौका पार नही होता
गर हो खुद पर विश्वास
तो कोई भी मंजिल दुर नही होता

एक पहचान हूँ~

एक वो वक़्त था और एक आज है
फ़र्क है, तब नादान थी अब ना अनजान हूँ
तब ना तनाव था पर अब हयात का चुनाव है
पहले गुमनाम थी और अब एक पहचान हूँ

सिखा दिया या कह लो सीख लिया है मैंने
खुद से खुद ही को नसीहत दिया है मैंने
इस असीम दुनिया का हसीन कोना हूँ मैं
जूँझते राही के ख़ज़ाने का सोना हूँ मैं

उस जलती ज्वाला की एक चिंगारी हूँ
गरजते बादलों की छिड़कती बूंदा-बांदी हूँ
ठंडे मट्ठे के प्याले में घुलती सी केसर हूँ
बंद कमरे की खिड़की से आती रोशनी हूँ

झरनों की गर्माहट और पत्तों पर शबनम हूँ
गुलदस्ते की आगोश में मरघूब सुगंध हूँ
हर काफ़िले की पनपती नाज़ हूँ मैं
अंबर में पंछियों के बीच बाज़ हूँ मैं

इबादत हूँ, फरियाद हूँ, चाहत हूँ, बुनियाद हूँ
ख्वाब हूँ, इंतजाम हूँ, नायाब हूँ, अंजाम हूँ
हर लफ्ज़ हर फैसले का आगाज़ हूँ
हज़ारों की भीड़ में, एक पहचान हूँ

जिदंगी

जिदंगी ज़रा यूं थमी सी लगती है,
आँखों में एक नमी- सी लगती है,
यूं तो काफी कुछ है पास मेरे,
फिर भी एक कमी सी लगती है,
कुछ है जो खो गया है,
या कुछ पाने की तमन्ना है,
दिल है सिर्फ उसी की सुनती हूँ,
उसमें भी खलबली सी लगती है,
कुछ है शायद जो भूल रहीं हूँ,
या कहीं यादों में झूल रही हूँ,
यूं तो छोडा़ है सब मैनें,
फिर भी जैसे,
अभी अभी सी लगती हूँ!!!!!

अलविदा

तुझे अलविदा कहने गयी हूँ,
जब ये ख्याल आया,
मेरी रुह का मेरे जिस्म से सवाल आया,
वो बोली क्या आवाज़ आ रही है,
कि तेरे संग वो भी जा रही है,
ये सुनकर जज़बातों में बवाल आया,
तुझे अलविदा कहने गयी हूँ,
जब ये ख्याल आया|
तुझे जाता देखकर जम सी गयी थी मैं,
टूटी बिखरी तुझे रोक न पायी,
मेरी मोहब्बत ने किस्मत से था धोखा खाया,
मैं मरकर अपनी चाहत को संभाल आयी,
तुझे अलविदा कहने गयी हूँ,
जब ये ख्याल आया!!!!!

Afsar Shaikh.

Hii i am afsar shaikh. i am student in Bsc MLT. I love writing my own thoughts. I have starter writing from past 1 year hope you all like it.

Mohabbat Aur Dosti Mein Faraq

Mohabbat aur dosti mein ye faraq hai ki
Mohabbat agar jaann leti hai
Toh dosti jaan deti hai
Mohabbat a gar Khushi deti hai toh dosti khushi ke peeche
chupi aansoo ki waja jaanti hai

Mohabbat agar saalon baad mile toh nazren chura leti hai lekin
agar dosti mile toh seene se laga leti hai
Mohabbat kehti hai tumhare bina zinda nahi reh sakta lekin
dosti kehti hai ki yaar mein toh tujhe marne hi nahi dunga

(2)

Nahi hota aasani se kissi per bharosa agar ho jaye toh usse
tutne na dena q ki
Bharosa woh nazuk shisha hai jo ek martaba tutt jaye toh phir
kabhi nahi judta or jud bhi jaye toh che hre doo hi nazar aate
hai

Jis Tarah

Qeemat paani ki nahi pyaas ki hoti hai
Qeemat maut ki nahi saans ki hoti hai
Or jis tarah dost toh bahut hote hai
Iss duniya mein lekin
Qeemat dosti ki nahi
Bharose ki hoti hai
Thik ussi tarah mohabbat toh har koi kar
Leta hai lekin Mohabbat
Mein qeemat zyada wafa ki hoti hai

Ek Tarfah Mohabbat

Bahut ajeeb hoti hai ek tarfah mohabbat jis mein na Izhar e
ishq hota hai or nahi iqrar e mohabbat
Jo baat na kabhi kahi gai ho dil woh sunta rehta hai
Bewaja khwaab bunta rehta hain naa jane kiski nazar lag jati
hai na kinara milta hai na thikana milta hai
Ek tarfah mohbbat mein
Na hi ye mumkin hai jo dil ne chaha hai woh mil jaye agar
umeed toote toh kya karein

Ek Tarfah Mohabbat Mein Joo

Khwaab dekhe woh haqiqat nahi ban pata hai
Dil darta hai Izhar-e-ishq ko ki agar qismat sath na de toh kya
karein bas yahi soch ke dil rota ki kahi se sabar mil jaye Aksar

Jo dil ke pass rehte hai wahi dil tod dete hai na jane q wafa ke
badle bewafai mil jaye

(5)

Jisse humsafar banana chahte hai kahi woh Anjan na ban jaye
jis mohbbat se ishq kiya kahi woh Izhar ke baad bejaan na
hojaye ye rishta
Khushi ke darwaze per kahi gam ke badal na chah jaye
Jis se mohabbat ki jaye uska sath paana aasaan nahi hota uske
dur chale jaane se ye dil kahi weeran na hojaye jo naseb mein
hi na likha ho woh kaise mil jaye
Ye mumkin toh nahi jo dil chaha hai woh mil jaye

Flairs and Glairs, a platform by a student for the students. We are esteemed youth struggling to carve out our path for our future and we follow a basic mindset Since everyone is not born with allround skills. Joining hands with people who are born to execute it with perfection is the best way to evolve. Self -Evolution is the need of the hour but, evolving as a community is what we strive for. The initiative as kickstarted by, Founder - Mr. Shubham Shah with the motive to utilize the skillset and talent of writing has now a team of 10+ people who are actively participating into newer forms of learning and discovering talents among youngsters. We Provide platform and services like Publishing opportunities, Open mics, Workshops, Hands-on training. Operating with Brand Name of Flairs and Glairs (Publication House), we offer the chance of elevating a passionate writer to an esteemed author   With Brand name Teekhe Zasbaaat. We bring to you an opportunity to get accustomed with the Public Speaking and Presenting of Thoughts along with r egular challenges to brush up your inking spirit.   The newest initiative to extend our services we introduced in a new writing Platform- The Glittering Fables and Ink Over Tears.

We Choose to Fly Like A Falcon than to be

a Leg Pulling Crab.

To Know More: Infoline – 7781900870
Mail Us At-
flairsandglairs@gmail.com / info@flairsandglairs.in
Or Visit is at
www.flairsandglairs.com / www.flairsandglairs.in
Social Handles- @flairsandglairs @teekhezasbaaat